D.W. THINKS BIG

D.W. THINKS BIG

Marc Brown

SCHOLASTIC INC.

New York Toronto London Auckland Sydney
Mexico City New Delhi Hong Kong Buenos Aires

For Stacy, the bride,
Chris, the groom,
and Eliza, the flower girl

ISBN 0-439-38433-8

12 11 10 9 8 7 6 5 4 3   2 3 4 5 6 7/0

Printed in the U.S.A.   23

First Scholastic printing, April 2002

Aunt Lucy was getting married in two hours.
Everyone was getting ready.
Arthur's job was to carry the wedding ring down the aisle.
He practiced with his mother's ring.
"Why can't I be in the wedding, too?" asked D.W.
"Why can't I carry the ring?"

"You're too little," said Arthur. "And, besides, the ring bearer is always a boy. Everyone knows that."
"Be careful with my ring!" called Mother.
"At least I'd be able to keep the ring on the pillow!" said D.W.

"Let's get a picture of Arthur in his new suit," said Father.
"Fix his tie, first," said Mother. "And put on your dress,
D.W., or we'll be late."

"Why can't I be the flower girl?" asked D.W.
"I can walk slowly. I know how to hold my dress out
and take tiny steps."

"Cousin Cora is the flower girl," said Mother.
"She's older," said Father.
"She's my age," said Arthur.

"Why does Arthur get to sit in the front seat?" asked D.W. on the way to the wedding.

"I have a very important job," said Arthur. "They can't get married without the ring."

"That's true," said Father. "But try not to be nervous."

"Maybe Cousin Cora will get nervous, too," said D.W. "Then I can be the flower girl."

But Cousin Cora wasn't nervous at all.
And she had on pink nail polish. And shoes with bows.
"See my new dress?" said Cora. "It's great for swirling."
"I have a new purse," said D.W.
"With thirty-one pennies inside."

But Cora wasn't listening.
She was too busy twirling and swirling.
"I'm so excited!" said Cora.

D.W. went to find Aunt Lucy. She was very busy.
"Next time you get married can I help?" asked D.W.
But with everyone talking Aunt Lucy couldn't hear D.W.

Finally D.W. just sat down and watched everyone
else get ready.
"Are you lost, little girl?" asked the photographer.
"I'm not little and I'm not lost!" said D.W.

"Hurry up, D.W.," said Mother.
"The wedding is about to begin."
"Good luck, Arthur," said Father.
"Don't forget to smile," said Grandma Thora.

The music began.

Cora started down the aisle, holding her dress out and taking tiny steps.

"Why is everyone crying?" asked D.W. "Are they sad?"

"No," said Mother. "They're crying because they're so happy."

Arthur walked down the aisle after Cora.
He remembered to smile.
But when he stopped to wave to D.W. the pillow tipped . . .
and the ring fell!

Arthur tried to catch it, but the ring began to roll — faster
and faster down the aisle . . .
right into a heating vent.

"Now everyone really has something to cry about!" said D.W.
"Relax," said Uncle Shelly. "I'll get it."
He opened the vent and looked in.
"It's a long way down!" he grunted. "I can't quite reach it."
"Let me try," said Arthur.

In he went.

"Your new suit!" cried Mother.

"Help!" cried Arthur. "I'm stuck!"

After they pulled Arthur out, Cora offered to try.

"I think we need someone smaller," said Uncle Shelly.

"I'm small enough," said D.W. "Hold my feet."
Down she went.
THUMP! CLANK! CLONK!

And up she came.
"I found it!" she called.
Everyone cheered.

The music began again.
This time it was D.W. who walked down the aisle.
Slowly, taking very tiny steps and careful to hold her dress
out, she carried the ring.
She only stopped to let the photographer take her picture.

Finally, she reached the bride and groom.
"Thanks, D.W.!" whispered Aunt Lucy. "We couldn't have
done it without you."
"I may be little," said D.W., "but sometimes I can be
a big help!"